TYRANNOSAURUS TIME

BY

JOANNE RYDER

ILLUSTRATED BY

MICHAEL ROTHMAN

MORROW JUNIOR BOOKS • NEW YORK

The author gratefully acknowledges the contribution of Armand Morgan, museum educator and illustrator, Yale Peabody Museum of Natural History, New Haven, Connecticut, to the preparation of this manuscript. She is also grateful to the scientists and writers who have contributed to the greater understanding of dinosaur life and particularly recommends *The Complete T. Rex,* by John R. Horner and Don Lessem (New York: Simon & Schuster, 1993).

Michael Rothman's daughter, Nyanza, and her friend Gary Goldfinger were the models for the children who appear in this book.

AUTHOR'S NOTE

Tyrannosaurus rex is believed to be one of the largest meat-eaters ever to have hunted on land. It was about forty feet in length, stood fifteen to eighteen feet tall on two muscular hind legs, and weighed about six tons. Up to sixty teeth lined its four-foot-long jaw, and some of those fearsome spikes, serrated and sawlike, were six inches long. Many scientists think *Tyrannosaurus rex* hunted as large cats do today, taking advantage of whatever feeding opportunities it could by preying on the unwary, the sick and injured, and the weakest young and old animals, as well as eating any dead animals it discovered.

Dinosaurs, large and small, flourished on earth for 160 million years. *Tyrannosaurus rex* lived at the end of the dinosaurs' reign, in a lush, warm Cretaceous world. It encountered massive plant-eating dinosaurs, such as the horned *Triceratops,* armored ankylosaurs, and the duckbill hadrosaurs, and other ancient creatures—giant winged pterosaurs, huge crocodiles, early salamanders, frogs, birds, and tiny mammals.

Scientists believe that about 65 million years ago many kinds of creatures died in a mass extinction. Perhaps a catastrophic event, such as an asteroid colliding with the earth, or a more gradual process, involving increased volcanic activity and shifting continents, caused changes in the climate and environment that led to the death of many animals on the land and in the sea.

Yet many scientists think there are dinosaurs living today. Birds may be the descendants of small theropod dinosaurs. And theropods, a diverse group of two-footed, meat-eating dinosaurs, also included gigantic *Tyrannosaurus rex,* with its birdlike feet and movements.

Scientists try to understand life on earth millions of years ago by discovering and deciphering the fossil remains of ancient plants and animals. Much of this ancient world—the color of dinosaur skin, for instance—is lost to us, and much we may never know. In this book, I try to present a reasonable picture of dinosaur life based on current scientific views. However, today's scientists often have differing ideas. And, as more fossil evidence is understood, some theories will prove to be more likely than others.

The setting for this book is the late Cretaceous period, some 65 to 67 million years ago, in what is now the western United States.

Acrylic paint was used for the full-color illustrations.
The text type is 14-point ITC Bookman Medium.

Published by Morrow Junior Books, a division of William Morrow and Company, Inc.
1350 Avenue of the Americas, New York, NY 10019 www.williammorrow.com

Printed in Singapore at Tien Wah Press.

1 3 5 7 9 10 8 6 4 2

Library of Congress Cataloging-in-Publication Data
Ryder, Joanne.
Tyrannosaurus time / Joanne Ryder; illustrated by Michael Rothman.
p. cm.—(Just for a day book)
Summary: A child is transformed into a Tyrannosaurus rex for a day and discovers what it is like to be a killing machine and one of the largest meat-eating animals to have hunted on land.
ISBN 0-688-13682-6 (trade)—ISBN 0-688-13683-4 (library)
1. Tyrannosaurus rex—Juvenile fiction. [1. Tyrannosaurus rex—Fiction.
2. Dinosaurs—Fiction.] I. Rothman, Michael, ill. II. Title. III. Series.
PZ7.10.3.R954Ty 1999 [E]—dc21 98-45236 CIP AC

Under the sky
under the earth
under the rock
dinosaurs sleep.

Bone turned to stone
whispers to you
of other worlds,
drawing your fingers
to brush away sand and rock.
You reach and rub
a curved dark dagger—
a giant's saw-edged tooth
still sharp enough
to prick your finger.

As you touch the past,
ancient dust and sand
whirl in the wind
hiding you,
changing you....
You are growing
taller and taller,
longer and longer.
You barely feel the sand
rushing, brushing
against your pebbly skin.

Unable to see or hear,
you call out,
your voice rumbling
roaring with the wind.
And...when the wind fades
and the dust drifts away,
you see your world
changed too....

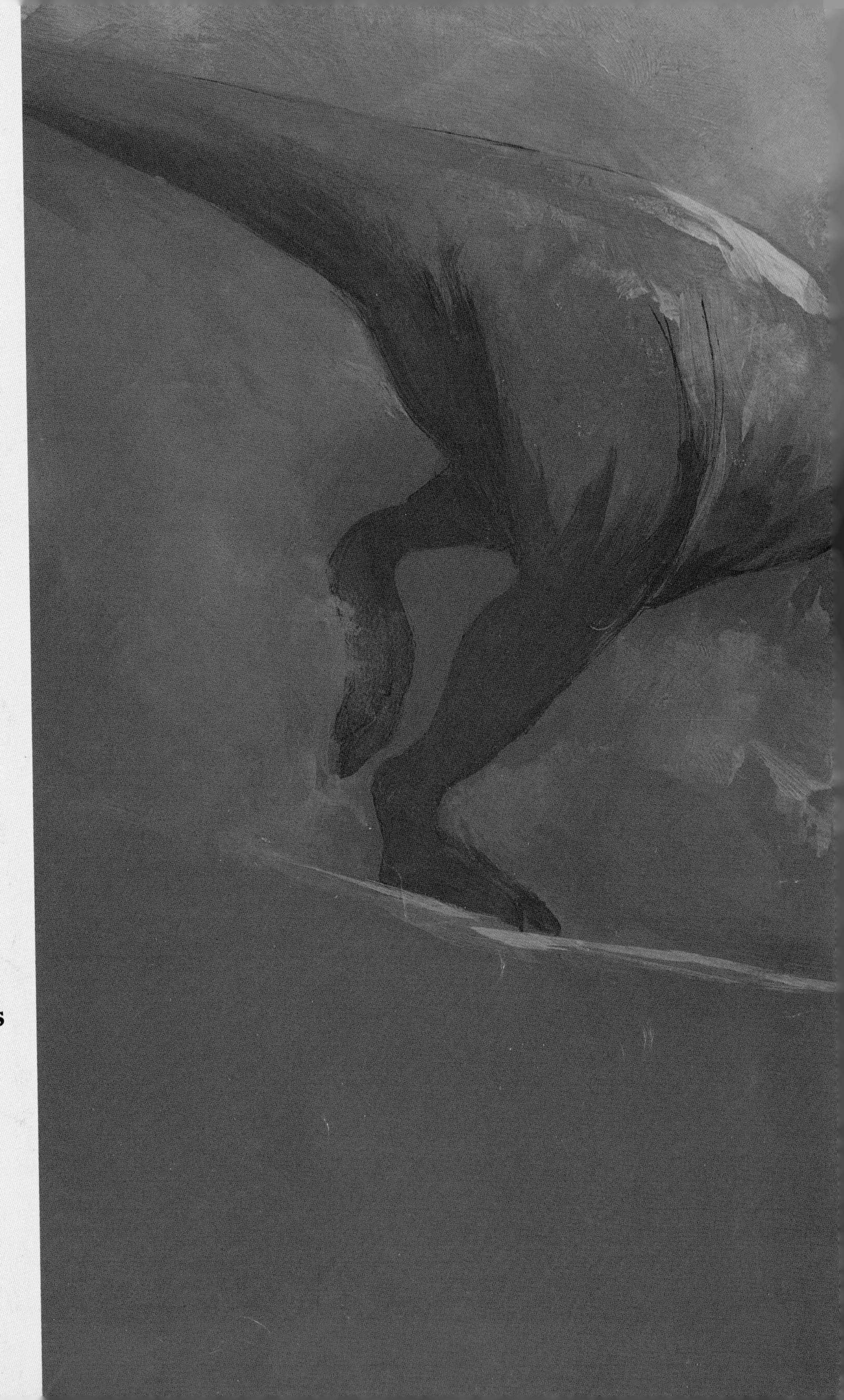

You are
Tyrannosaurus rex,
ruler of a warm
and ancient land
of green plains,
towering trees,
and flowering woods.
In the distance,
volcanoes rumble
where mountains
are growing tall.

You are a giant,
shaking the earth
with every step
as small ones
chatter and scatter,
scramble and leap,
fleeing from you.
Then...silently, swiftly
a broad shadow races
across the ground,
racing *toward* you....

Another giant—
exploring, soaring—
glides over your head,
her wide, pointed wings
blocking the sun.
You stretch
higher and higher,
teeth bared.
Two giants stare,
watching each other,
till she turns
with the wind,
rising far
beyond your reach.

You are a giant,
striding boldly
on two strong legs,
balancing
your heavy body,
your huge head
tilted low in front,
your tail stretched
long and high behind.
Your birdlike feet
leave narrow trails
of three-toed prints
in the soft mud
as you walk,
as you stalk,
as you run.

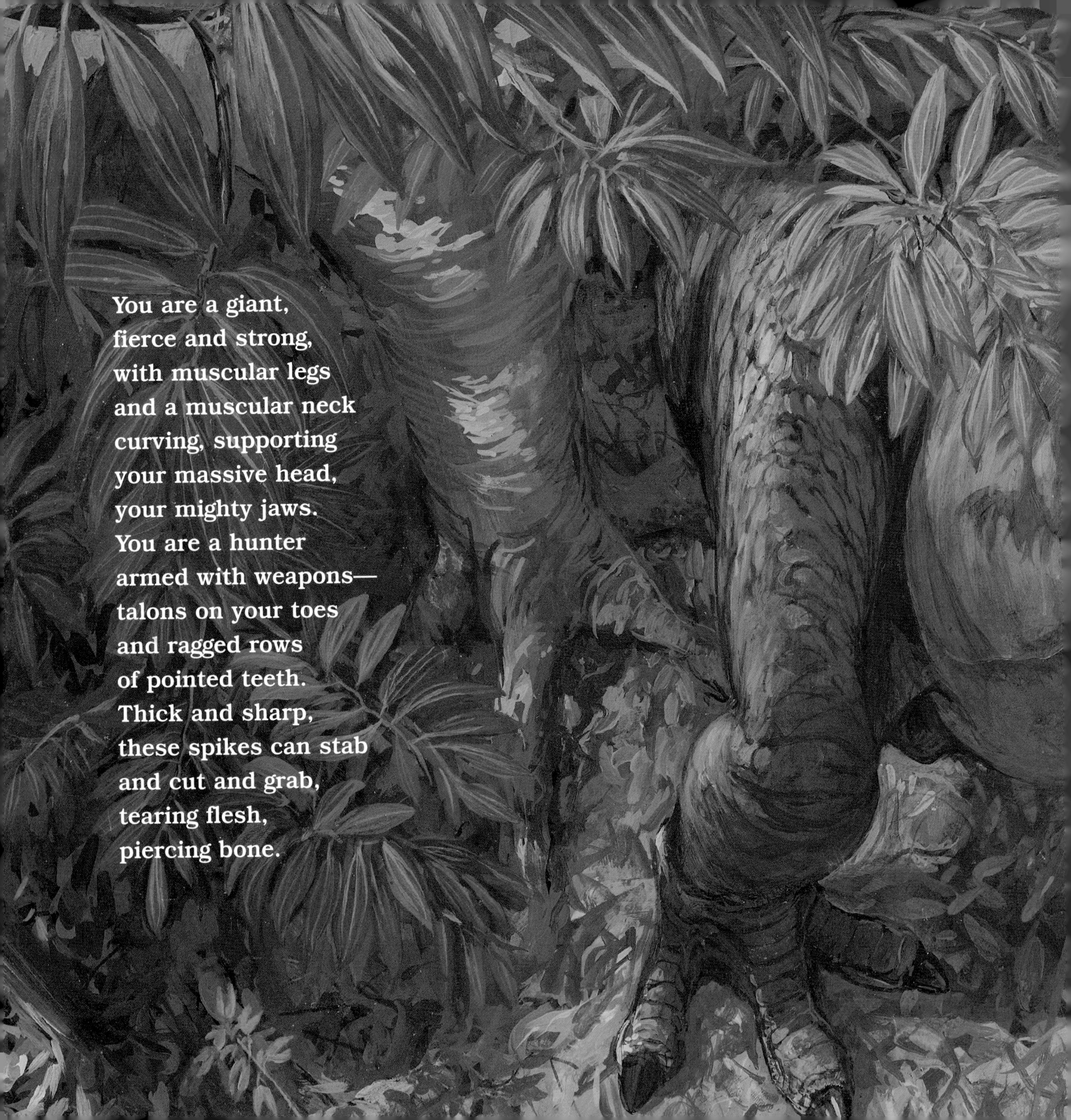

You are a giant,
fierce and strong,
with muscular legs
and a muscular neck
curving, supporting
your massive head,
your mighty jaws.
You are a hunter
armed with weapons—
talons on your toes
and ragged rows
of pointed teeth.
Thick and sharp,
these spikes can stab
and cut and grab,
tearing flesh,
piercing bone.

Alert and watchful,
you face the wind,
seeking, sniffing
the scents of others.
You listen—
hearing, tracking
dinosaurs calling,
dinosaurs mingling.
Hungry herds
grazing on the
greening shrubs
follow the trails
of leaves and flowers—
and you follow them.

Thirsty dinosaurs
drift toward the river.
You watch
the young ones
dip their flat heads
in the cool water.
Broad-beaked eaters
bend down,
nipping buds,
chewing twigs,
grinding their food
with hundreds of teeth.
You wait
as still as a tree,
as quiet as a stone,
but the wind shifts,
dancing around you,
carrying your
scent to them.

A tall one
snorts,
puffing,
inflating
his face,
roaring
a warning—
danger...
danger.
Dinosaurs flee,
sensing, knowing
you are too close
for them to stay.

You are a giant
stalking giants,
a sly shadow
waiting within shadows
as you spy
three-horned dinosaurs
wrestling for power.
Their heads lock—
pushing, testing
who is fiercer,
who is stronger.

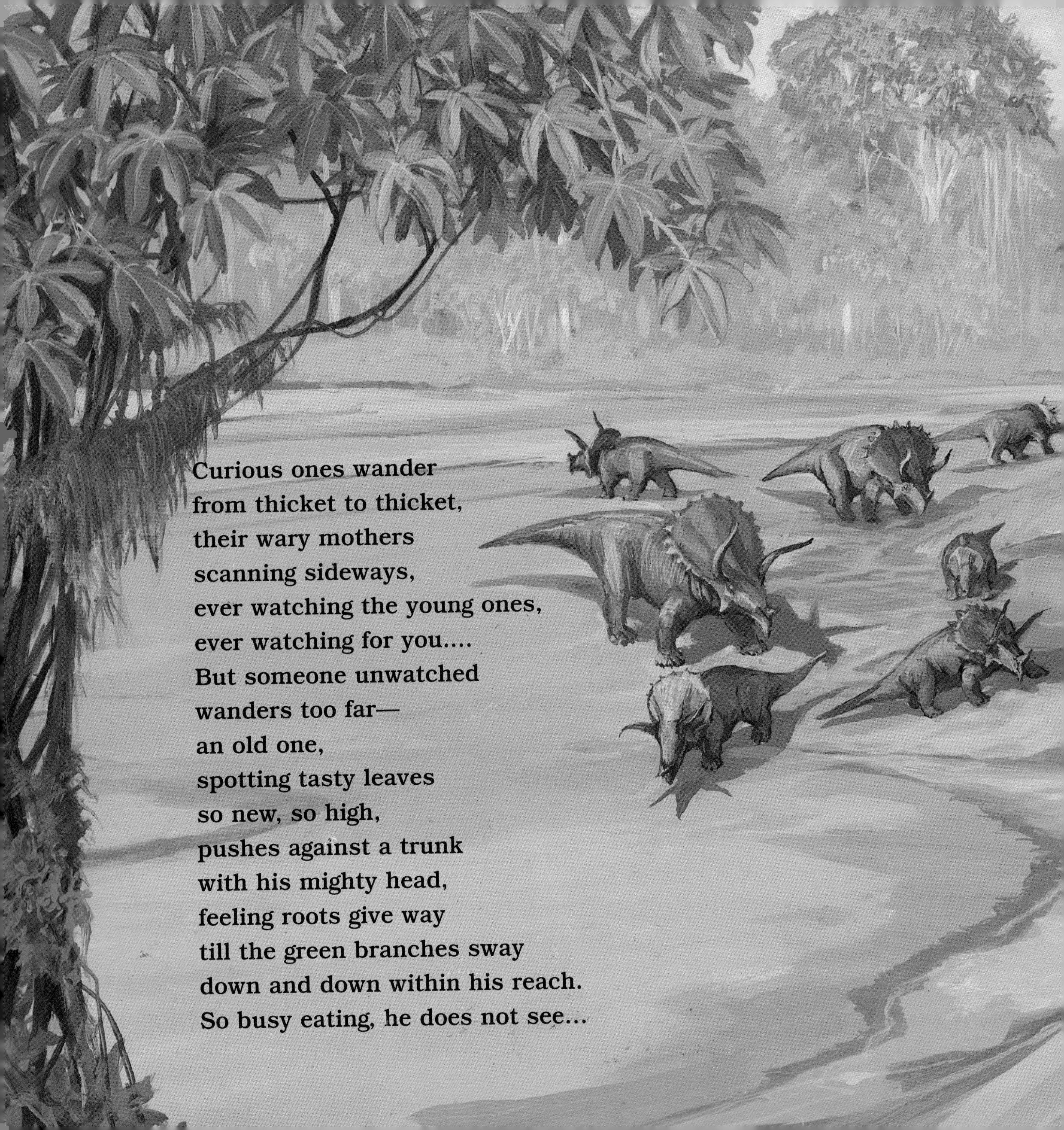

Curious ones wander
from thicket to thicket,
their wary mothers
scanning sideways,
ever watching the young ones,
ever watching for you....
But someone unwatched
wanders too far—
an old one,
spotting tasty leaves
so new, so high,
pushes against a trunk
with his mighty head,
feeling roots give way
till the green branches sway
down and down within his reach.
So busy eating, he does not see...

You burst
from the shadows,
charging, lunging,
mouth open wide.
Your eyes staring
straight ahead,
you keep him in sight,
judging the distance
between him and you
shrinking, shrinking
until he feels
the ground quivering
from your heavy footsteps—
too late!

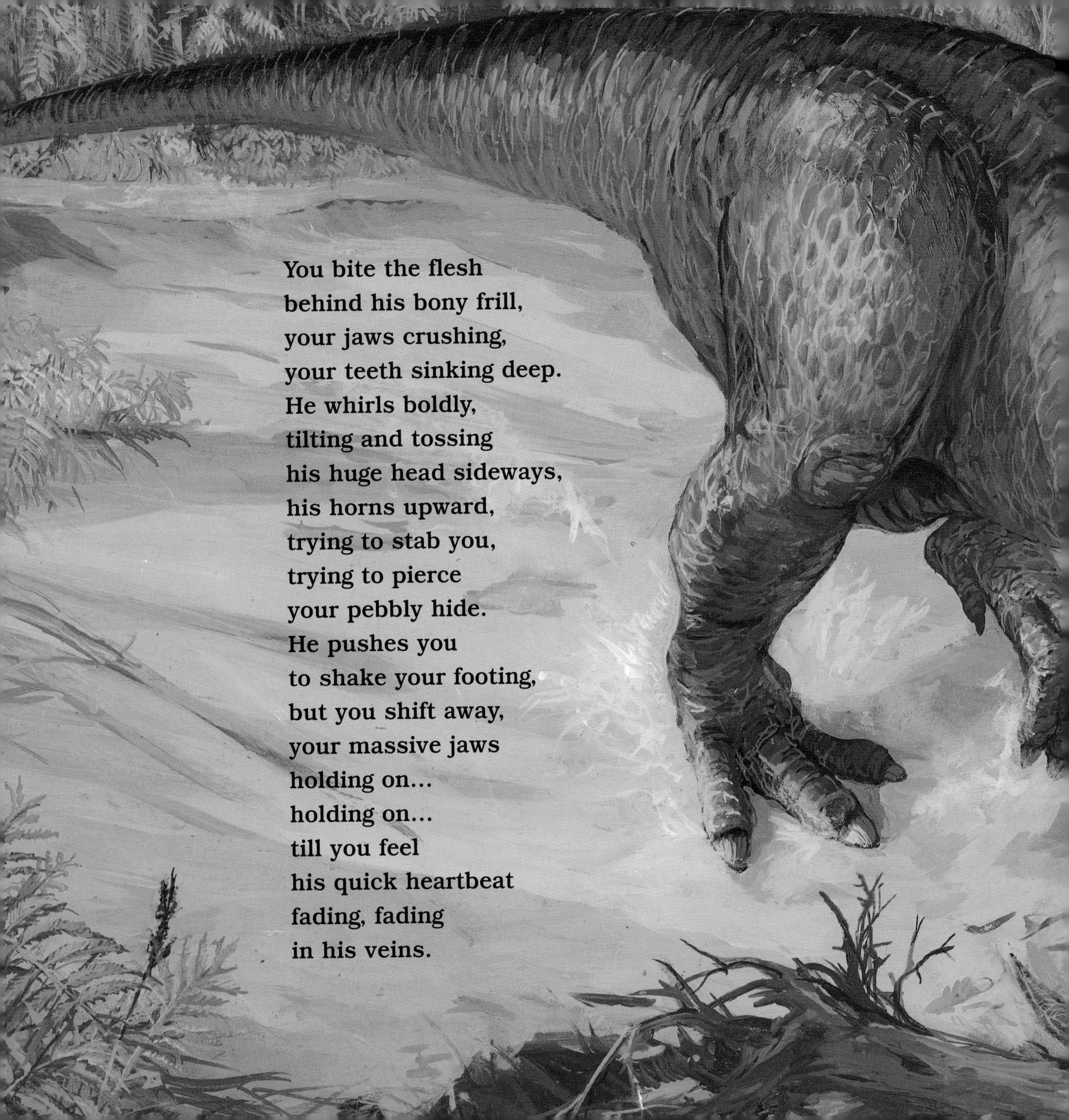

You bite the flesh
behind his bony frill,
your jaws crushing,
your teeth sinking deep.
He whirls boldly,
tilting and tossing
his huge head sideways,
his horns upward,
trying to stab you,
trying to pierce
your pebbly hide.
He pushes you
to shake your footing,
but you shift away,
your massive jaws
holding on...
holding on...
till you feel
his quick heartbeat
fading, fading
in his veins.

You eat and eat,
your belly swelling,
as the sun slips past
volcanoes glowing
in the distance.
Dark clouds rise high,
and your chest tightens
with the bitter scent
of ashes blowing,
blowing toward you.

You are the last
of a long line of giants.
Something is going
to change your world.
Something will end
the mild days
when the dinosaurs ruled.
And as the light fades,
a giant's footsteps echo,
pounding, pounding
beneath you
as you race
in the darkness,
leaping through time,
changing again....

You are
a thinker,
a dreamer,
gazing high
watching a fireball
flash across the sky.
And you wonder:
How... Why...
did the dinosaurs die?
Softly you walk
above the giants,
who roared
and who ruled,
and who rest
with the answers
tucked in the
rocks below.

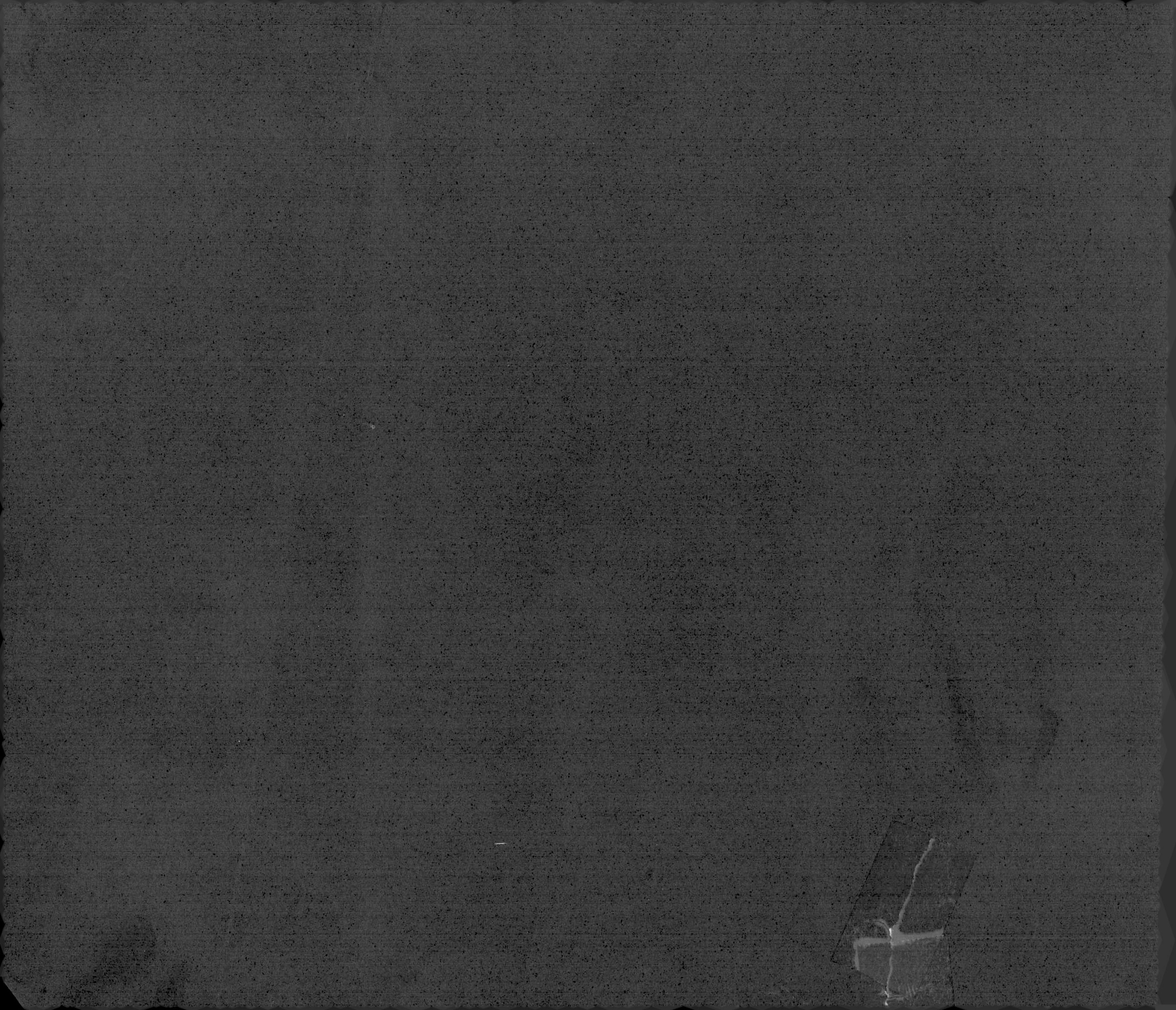

A Children's Zoo

by Tana Hoban

a division of
William Morrow & Company, Inc.,
1350 Avenue of the Americas,
New York, NY 10019.
Manufactured in China.
First Edition

20 19 18

Library of Congress
Cataloging in Publication Data

Hoban, Tana.
A children's zoo.
Summary: Color photographs of animals are accompanied by several descriptive words, e.g. tall, spotted, silent giraffe.
1. Animals—Juvenile literature.
[1. Animals] I. Title.
QL49.H674 1985
591 84-25318
ISBN 0-688-05202-9
ISBN 0-688-05204-5 (lib. bdg.)

Especially for Kirk and Oliver

black
white
waddles

PENGUIN

big
smooth
swims

HIPPOPOTAMUS

striped
black and white
gallops

ZEBRA

white
big
growls

POLAR BEAR

sleek
black
swims

SEA LION

strong
shaggy
roars

LION

red
blue
squawks

PARROT

gray
wrinkled
trumpets

ELEPHANT

black
white
furry

PANDA

tall
spotted
silent

GIRAFFE

A Children's Zoo

		Where do they come from?	Where do they live?	What do they eat?
PENGUINS		Antarctica, Australia, Africa, South America, New Zealand, Galapagos Islands	by the sea	fish
HIPPOPOTAMUSES		Africa	near rivers and swamps	vegetation
ZEBRAS		Africa	in woods and mountains	vegetation
POLAR BEARS		the Arctic	on ice floes and shores	fish and meat
SEA LIONS		the Pacific and Atlantic Oceans	on ice floes and shores	fish
LIONS		Africa, Asia	on the plains	meat
PARROTS		Africa, Asia, Australia, New Zealand	in jungles	vegetation
ELEPHANTS		Africa, Asia	in forests and on the plains	vegetation
PANDAS		Asia	in forests and mountains	vegetation and meat
GIRAFFES		Africa	in the bush	vegetation
KODIAK BEARS (cover)		North America	in the Northern wilderness	fish and meat